Longman Reading World at home

KV-191-877

Here is a story called

The two friends

A "what do you think?" story

written by Pat Edwards
illustrated by Katy Sleight

and this is the way it goes...

Once upon a time,
there were two friends called
1 Brenda and Bruce
2 Cornelius and Cyril
3 Isabella and Ivy
(What do you think?)

3

One day they
1 walked along the road
   to town
2 ran through the trees
3 skipped along the path
(What do you think?)

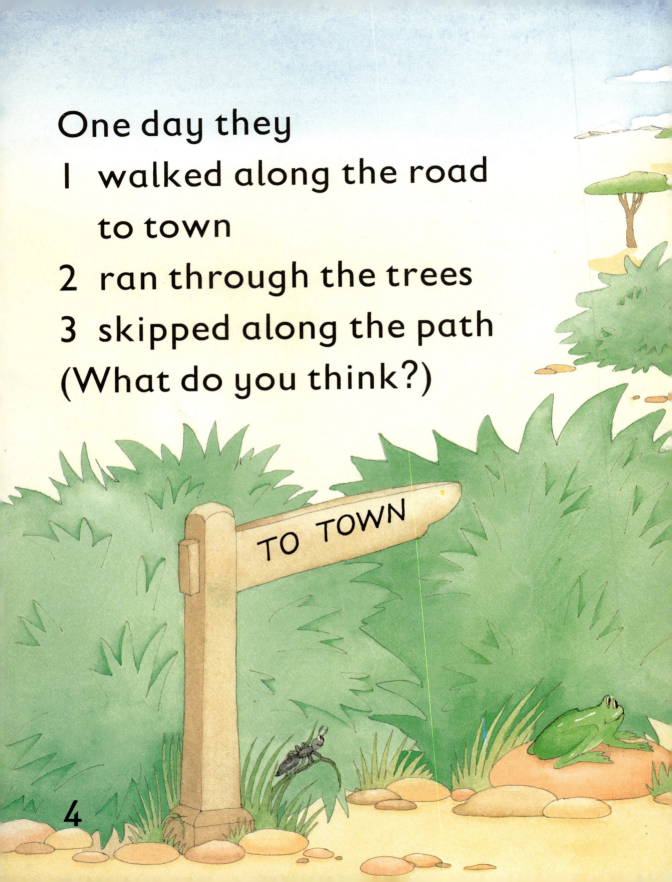

TO TOWN

4

5

As they went along they sang

1 Who's afraid of the
   big, bad cat?
2 Hickory, dickory, dock
3 Pussy cat, pussy cat, where
   are you now?
(What do you think?)

When they came to the river
they found a boat,
so they decided to
go and visit their old friend
1 Arthur
2 Wilma
3 Gerry
(Who do you think?)

It was lovely out on the river and they
1 sang more songs
2 told each other stories
3 asked each other riddles
(What do you think?)

They were so busy
they didn't notice the hole
in the bottom of the boat
till the water got up to their
1 knees
2 tummy buttons
3 chins
(Where do you think?)

12

13

1 "Help! Help!"
2 "What will we do?"
3 "How dreadful!"
 cried the two friends.
(What do you think?)

16

"Hold on," someone called.
"I'll help you."
It was
1 Claudine Crocodile
2 Charlie Cat
(Who do you think?)

Soon the two soggy friends
were safe on the river bank.

19

"Glad I could help you," said
1 Claudine with a wicked grin
2 Charlie with a nasty smile
(Who did you say?)

And before anyone could
blink an eyelash
or wiggle a whisker,
1 Charlie took them off to
    eat for his tea
2 they had scampered off
    home as fast as they could go
3 Claudine ate them both
(What do you think?)

22

They were delicious.

Pat your head,
rub your tum,
that's the lot—
book's all done!